DREAMWORKS
Trolls
WORLD TOUR

By David Lewman
Illustrated by Alan Batson and Fabio Laguna

A GOLDEN BOOK · NEW YORK

rhcbooks.com
ISBN 978-0-593-12791-9 (trade) — ISBN 978-0-593-12792-6 (ebook)
Printed in the United States of America
10 9 8 7 6 5 4 3 2 1

One bright and sunny morning, Queen Poppy woke up ready for another super-fun day of dancing, singing, and hugging with her fellow happy Trolls!

Suddenly, she heard Guy Diamond calling.

POPPY, come quick! It's an EMERGENCY!

Poppy rushed to Guy Diamond.

What's wrong?

I'm having a BABY!

Everyone's eyes grew wide with surprise
as an egg popped out of his hair. It cracked
open, revealing a glittery baby Troll!

Singing and dancing in an explosion of glitter and
megastar attitude, the newest Troll introduced himself
as **TINY DIAMOND.**

Poppy was excited. She thought Tiny Diamond was
AWESOME! And all the Trolls thought his cool rap
and hip dance moves were over-the-top!

Overcome with emotion, Branch decided to finally tell Poppy that he loved her. But right at that moment, Biggie yelled, **"HELP! I'M BEING ATTACKED BY A MONSTER!"**

The "monster" turned out to be a strange flying critter carrying an envelope addressed to Queen Poppy. She opened it and found a party invitation from someone named Barb, who said she was Queen of the Rocker Trolls.

"Rocker Trolls?" Poppy asked, puzzled. "What are Rocker Trolls?"

Poppy hurried to her father, King Peppy, for an explanation. King Peppy sighed. He had always known this day would come. He showed her and Branch an ancient scroll about the other kinds of Trolls in the world, including Rocker Trolls.

"Other kinds of Trolls?" Poppy said, excited. "That's great! The more Trolls, the merrier!"

King Peppy disagreed. "Not great," he said. "They sing differently, and they dance differently!"

King Peppy opened to a map. "There are six tribes of Trolls," he said. "Each tribe is named for its favorite music: the Rocker Trolls, the Techno Trolls, the Classical Trolls, the Country Western Trolls, the Funk Trolls, and us, the Pop Trolls. Each tribe has a powerful musical string, from which all the tribe's music flows!"

TROLLS KINGDOM

LONES

VIBE CITY

BERGENTOWN

"Wow," Poppy said, amazed.
"Where's OUR string?"

King Peppy showed Poppy and
Branch their musical string, which
was hidden behind a waterfall.
"The string MUST be kept safe,"
King Peppy warned, "or
legend has it that we
Pop Trolls will lose
ALL
our music!"

Despite his warning, Poppy was determined to unite all the Trolls. She sent a letter to Barb and prepared to fly in a giant balloon.

"I get it now!" she told Branch. "Queen Barb wants to bring all the Trolls together! I'm saying **YES** to her party invitation! And I can't stay home when there's a world of new Trolls out there!"

"That's a terrible idea," Branch grumbled. "But I'm coming with you."

Poppy and Branch climbed into a colorful balloon named Sheila B. "I'm so excited!" Poppy squealed. "Flying off to meet other Trolls!"

"But your dad said the other Trolls are different from us!" Branch reminded her.

"They're still Trolls!" Poppy argued, with her usual upbeat attitude. "Differences don't matter!"

From behind a bush, Cooper watched the balloon rise into the sky. "Different kinds of Trolls," he said to himself softly. "I wonder if Poppy and Branch will find any Trolls like me."

Cooper crept forward to get a closer look at the old scroll. He found a picture of a Funk Troll and gasped. **"This one looks just like me!** We even have the same HAT!"

Closing the scroll, Cooper decided to set off on his own to search for Trolls like himself.

Meanwhile, up in the balloon, Poppy heard snoring. She lifted a tarp and found . . . Biggie and Mr. Dinkles! Biggie had climbed into the balloon to sample the cotton candy, gumdrops, and other goodies that Poppy had brought along as a present for Queen Barb.

Just then, Branch spotted what appeared to be the smoking remains of the Classical Trolls' town.

They landed as quickly as possible, and soon met Pennywhistle, who sadly explained that the ruins were all that was left of Symphonyville.

"Who did this?" Poppy asked.

"Queen Barb and the Rocker Trolls," Pennywhistle answered, shocking Poppy with the news.

What Poppy didn't realize was that Queen Barb wanted to bring all the Trolls' music together—but *her* way!

"Let's go over the plan again," Barb said to the other Rocker Trolls, including her dad, King Thrash. "We go on a World Tour to bring all the Trolls and their strings to Volcano Rock City . . . where I'll use the six strings to play the ultimate power chord so that ALL Trolls will ROCK!"

The Rocker Trolls cheered!

. . . **DESTROY ALL SIX STRINGS!** It was the only way to stop Barb. "Are you CRAZY?" Barb screamed. "You've destroyed MUSIC!"

While Barb raged, Poppy gathered all the Trolls to sing together. They didn't need their strings! The six tribes of Trolls may have been different from each other in little ways, but it takes different voices to make great harmony. And they all loved making music! Nothing could change that.

The Trolls sang together in perfect harmony. Barb scowled, but even she couldn't help herself. She started singing, too!

When their beautiful song ended, Branch shouted for everyone to hear: **"POPPY, I LOVE YOU!"**

"I love you, too, Branch," Poppy replied, her face lighting up with the biggest, brightest smile ever.

All the Trolls cheered. It had been the most Troll-tastic day on record . . . and with everyone in harmony, there were sure to be more!

Poppy stared at the ruins of Symphonyville. "So Queen Barb doesn't want to unite us. She wants to destroy us! We've got to stop her!" she said.

Biggie shuddered. "That sounds scary!"

Poppy linked her pinky with Biggie's and promised to protect him. Then they headed off to Lonesome Flats to get help from the Country Western Trolls.

Back on her tour bus, Barb received Poppy's friendly response to her invitation. The Rocker thought Poppy was making fun of her, with all her talk of becoming "best friends." Furious, Queen Barb ordered bounty hunters—Chaz the Smooth Jazz Troll, the Reggaeton Trolls, and the K-Pop Gang—to catch Queen Poppy.

When Poppy, Branch, and Biggie reached Lonesome Flats,
they heard Delta Dawn and her fellow Country Western Trolls
singing a sad song. "They must not know that music's supposed
to make you happy," Poppy said. She decided to show them . . .
by singing a totally rad greatest-hits **POP MEDLEY!**

SLAM!

Delta Dawn and Growley Pete threw the Pop Trolls into a jail cell and locked the door!

"I want you to sit in there and think about what you just did," Delta Dawn scolded, still unable to believe what she had just heard. "That was a crime against music!"

As soon as Delta Dawn was gone, Branch pulled his trusty travel shovel out of his hair and started to dig an escape tunnel. **CRASH!** Suddenly, the outside wall of the jail collapsed!

A Country Western Troll had pulled it down. "Name's Hickory," he said. "It's not right to toss you in jail just 'cause your music's different. Let's skedaddle!"

Hickory and the Pop Trolls dashed out of Lonesome Flats. But the Country Western Trolls saw them leaving and dashed after them.

The Pop Trolls ran right off the edge of a cliff and plunged into a raging river!

SPLASH!

The Pop Trolls pulled themselves onto the riverbank, soaking wet but okay. Even though Branch was suspicious of Hickory, Poppy thanked him and gave him some gumdrops.

After telling them the river was the quickest route to the Funk Trolls, Hickory started building a raft.

As the friends floated down the river, they spotted one of Barb's bounty hunters! Chaz started playing some smooth jazz music. It hypnotized Poppy, Branch, Biggie, and Mr. Dinkles.

"That music," Biggie droned. "So . . . smooooooth . . ."

WHACK! Hickory knocked Chaz away, breaking his spell.

"How'd you resist his music?" Poppy asked.

Hickory took gumdrops out of his ears. "Gumdrops—delicious *and* soundproof!"

Scared by the bounty hunter,
Biggie decided to go home.

"You didn't keep us safe!" he
said to Poppy. "What kind of
queen breaks a pinky promise?"

As she watched Biggie ride
away on Mr. Dinkles, Poppy
felt terrible.

Meanwhile, in another part of the hot desert, Cooper tried to drink water at an oasis, but it turned out to be a mirage. *I'm done for!* he thought. Suddenly, a bubble floated down and lifted him into the air!

The bubble carried him into a big spaceship. **POP!** The bubble burst and Cooper landed on the floor. He looked up at two shadowy figures. A kind female voice said, "I think our search is finally over!"

Poppy spotted the spaceship from their raft on the river. Excited, she pulled out her map of the Troll lands.

"That's Vibe City!" she said. "I think we've found the Funk Trolls! But how are we supposed to get up there?"

FWOOM! A bright beam of light shot down from Vibe City. One by one, Poppy, Branch, and Hickory were pulled up into the ship with colorful bubbles!

In the spaceship, Poppy was shocked to see . . . COOPER!

"Poppy," he said, grinning, "meet Queen Essence, King Quincy, and Prince D—my parents and my twin brother!"

"You mean you're a Funk Troll?" Branch asked.

"Yup!" Cooper said proudly. "But my egg fell out of the nest and got lost, so I was raised by Pop Trolls! My parents searched and searched but couldn't find me."

Just then, a siren went off.

"The Rocker Trolls are attacking!" King Quincy shouted. "Prepare for battle!"

"I'm going to make sure you get to safety!" Cooper said, playing notes on a keyboard. Bubbles carried the Pop Trolls and Hickory away from Vibe City.

"But I want to help!" Poppy cried.

When they reached the ground, Branch thought they should hurry home to protect their string and their friends. But Poppy said they should stay and fight the Rocker Trolls.

"You never listen to me!" Branch said. "So why do I care more about you than anyone else in the world?" Upset, he ran off into the woods. Stunned, Poppy watched him go.

In the forest, the bounty hunters grabbed Branch and took him to **Volcano Rock City,** where Barb was gathering the Trolls from all six lands!

Poppy told Hickory that Branch didn't need to go home to protect their string, because she had hidden it in her hair.

"See?" she said, pulling it out.

"Put it away!" Hickory begged. "And run as fast as you can."

"Too late!" Barb crowed, swooping down and snatching the string. **"VOLCANO ROCK CITY, HERE WE COME!"**

Barb flew Poppy and all the other Trolls to her rock arena.

"Now," she gloated, "I'll play the ultimate power chord! All Trolls will love Rock . . . **AND ROCK WILL RULE!"**

While Barb was putting the last string in her guitar, Poppy used her hair to pick the lock on her cage and escape so she could . . .